**PLATEOSAURUS**

**TRICERATOPS**

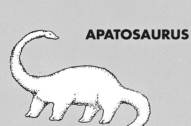

**APATOSAURUS**

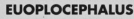

**COMPSOGNATHUS**

**EUOPLOCEPHALUS**

**CORYTHOSAURUS**

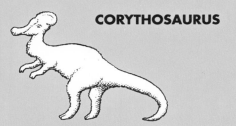

**DEINONYCHUS**

# Peter Sís

# DINOSAUR!

**Greenwillow Books,** *An Imprint of HarperCollinsPublishers*

**For the dinosaurs at the American Museum of Natural History, New York City**

Gouache paints, watercolors, and pen and ink were used for the full-color art. Dinosaur! Copyright © 2000 by Peter Sís. Printed in Singapore by Tien Wah Press. All rights reserved. http://www.harperchildrens.com

Sís, Peter. Dinosaur! / pictures by Peter Sís. p. cm. "Greenwillow Books." Summary: While taking a bath, a young boy is joined by all sorts of dinosaurs. ISBN 0-688-17049-8 [1. Dinosaurs—Fiction. 2. Baths—Fiction. 3. Imagination—Fiction. 4. Stories without words.] I. Title. PZ7.S6219Di 2000 [E]—dc21 99-32923 CIP

1 2 3 4 5 6 7 8 9 10 First Edition

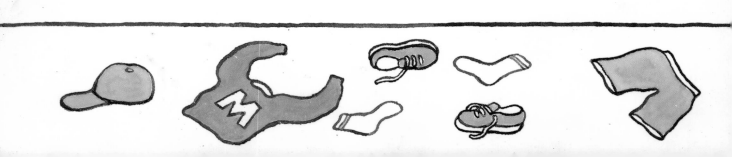

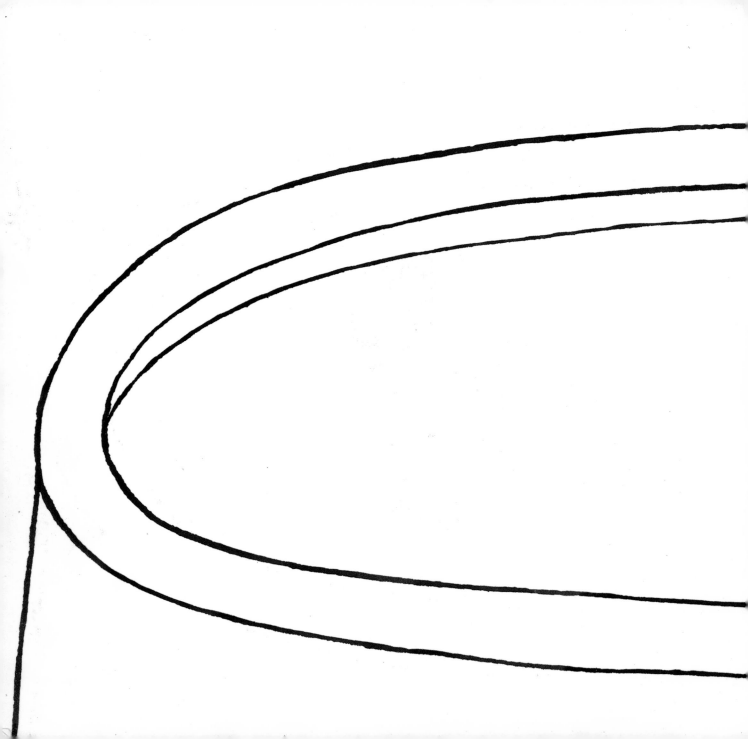

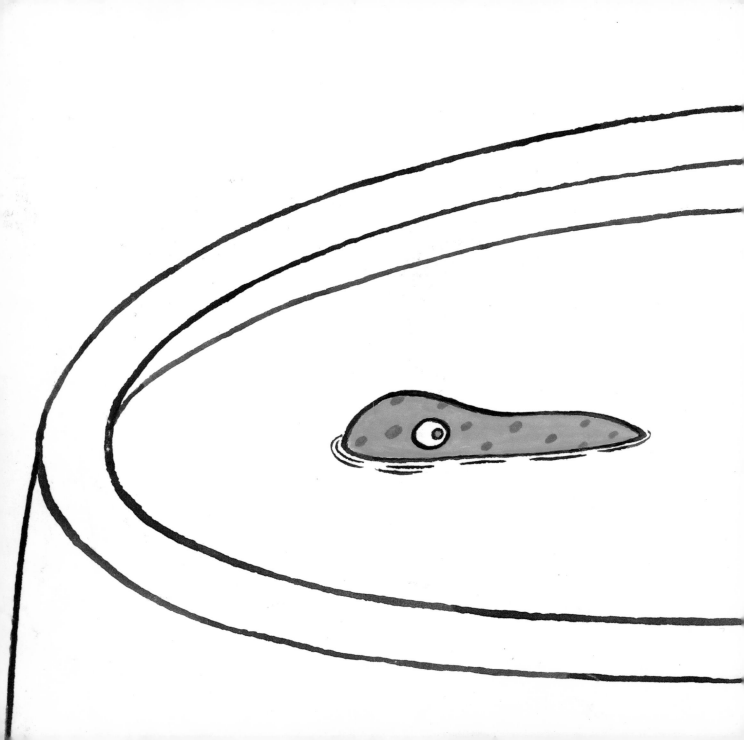

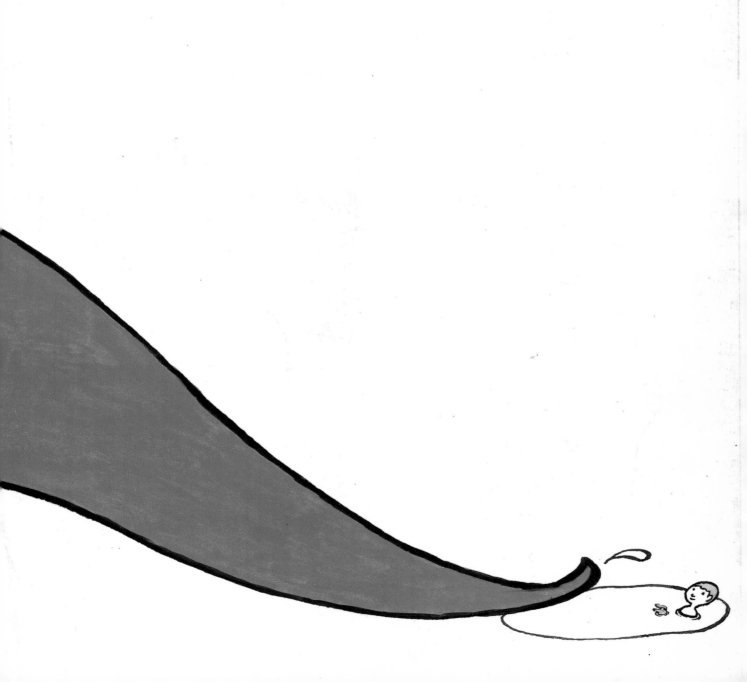

**STEGOSAURUS**

**SAUROLOPHUS**

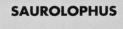

**IGUANODON**

**PTERANODON**

**TYRANNOSAURUS**

**CAMPTOSAURUS**